Flash Fiction

2011 Anthology

Pen Press

First published in Great Britain by Pen Press

All paper used in the printing of this book has been made from wood grown in managed, sustainable forests.

ISBN13: 978-1-78003-311-2

Printed and bound in the UK
Pen Press is an imprint of
Indepenpress Publishing Limited
25 Eastern Place
Brighton
BN2 1GJ

A catalogue record of this book is available from the British Library

Cover design by Jacqueline Abromeit

www.authoressentials.com
0845 519 3977

'Sometimes I've believed as many as six impossible things before breakfast'

Lewis Carroll, *Alice in Wonderland*

Introduction

We at Author Essentials deal with writers and authors every day. People come to us from all walks of life with books that range from humorous, to downright brilliant. In summer 2011, we thought it was time we gave something back to the writing community, so we contacted Indepenpress – an independent publisher that is passionate about finding new writing talent.

The result was the first annual Author Essentials Flash Fiction competition – 1st prize an outstanding publishing contract to give a break to real writing talent that deserves to be in print. At the time, we had no idea what we would discover.

The response we had from writers was fantastic - not just in the number of entries, but also the quality of the writing. As more and more entries came in, we found it increasingly hard to narrow it down! It seemed a shame that many of the stories would not find their place in print. And so, we compiled a list of the very best of the entries this year and popped them in this book for the whole world to enjoy.

These stories range in genre, length and style. Some were chosen for their creativity and descriptive content, others for the impact they had over such a small amount of words. Some we loved because of the elaborate styling, some because they were perfectly simplistic. Sweet, savoury and everything in between – this anthology has it all.

So, carry this book in your handbag, prop it open on the breakfast table and let these stories from writers and authors from all walks of life tickle your taste buds and make you hungry for more!

Contents

Flash Fiction

Short Stories

ICARUS GETS HIS WINGS

Steve Wade

Gorgeously plumaged in a regal red, redder than the tulips planted outside his aviary, and a blue more blue than midday shadows cast on fallen snow, Icarus, the crimson rosella parakeet, flicked seeds through the mesh-wire of his home to his feathered admirers. Gathered round were blue tits, gold finches, great tits and chaffinches.

The most beautiful bird they'd ever seen, they chirped and whistled. *In sky or land no bird could match his beauty*. Some went further: *And was he not more striking than the handsomest dog fox? - And more majestic, too, than the noblest stag? Why even the sun, aflame in the kingfisher-blue sky, lost his radiance when Icarus appeared*, they said.

On cue, the sun drifted behind a solitary cloud.

Gracefully, Icarus unfurled his wings from behind his back, stretched them sideways, though not fully, tipped his head skyward and squawked in self-satisfaction.

To please Icarus further, the flocks toned down their flying skills to compensate for his single flaw, his clipped wings. But he had a surprise for them - for later.

Icarus dipped his beak into the seed feeder, picked up a single seed, and, using his stubby tongue, flicked it to the crowd.

But when Icarus emerged from the feeder with another seed, the feathered flock, responding to a familiar, cackled warning, exploded like a puffball into the golden privet hedging and the pear tree in full white blossom.

The magpies were here.

With a vulgarity Icarus found distasteful, the magpies nonetheless knew their place. And, despite their inelegance, how could he deny that their voice was special: a staccato song encased in a timbre and tone not unlike his - though his voice, of course, had far more depth and range.

And how was His Royal Highness this bright morning? Did His Serene Highness have a comfortable night? No feathers out of place, one of them said. There followed a general, communal cackle, just as Icarus expected.

In response, Icarus squawked twice in a pitch so high and so loud, the magpies, to a bird, visibly flinched.

The tribe of magpies recovered their composure quickly. Feed us, Sir. Feed us, great Prince Icarus.

By the beak-full, he scooped up the seed, shook his head this way and that, allowing the seed to spill through the mesh-wire like water from the rose head on the end of the hose held by the man when he watered the tulips.

Picturing the man in his head caused Icarus to step from one foot to the other on his perch in excited anticipation. The sun had now climbed high above the pear tree. The man would soon be here.

In a wing-beat he arrived.

They'd be back, the magpies told him. Off they flew to the chimney tops and waited.

Using his beak and feet, Icarus clambered down the aviary's mesh-wire front to greet the man at the aviary entrance.

With a triumphant squawk, Icarus flapped madly passed him and through the entrance, and pulled himself towards the sky. Instantly he felt the warm air play about his plumage, tickle his face and, like a flock of amorous beaks, probe and scratch beneath his breast feathers.

He'd done it. Kept the sprouting plumes a secret from man and bird, till his wings were air-worthy. Now what did they make of him?

Below him, on the roofs and chimneys, in the cherry-blossoms, the crab-apples and the hawthorns, the flocks were thickening.

Exhilarated and exhausted, Icarus finally came to rest in the highest branch of the pear tree, where he squawked a humble 'Thank you', closed his eyes and bowed.

A charm of goldfinches and a parcel of linnets were the first to fall upon him. Who did he think he was, they chirped, with his gaudy coat and twisted beak, flying freely as though he were normal? They jabbed at his eyes and feet with their sharp and pointy beaks.

The murder of magpies followed the finches. The finches made way, as the magpies chuckled and jeered while hammering Icarus with their heavy bills until he fell from the tree.

He landed next to the feet of the shouting and flightless man.

EYES WIDE OPEN

Julia Millen

I'll be glad when the funeral is over. Caithlin wanted a burial, as was the way back home. A joint grave she said, together in birth and in death. But she was always tight with her money so I persuaded her a cremation, it'd be cheaper and Father O'Rouke said it was fine by the church, so for once I got my own way. My cousin Rory was all for a vigil but I said 'twould be spooky - a body lying out all night in a church. 'Twouldn't be safe in Tottenham," I insisted, and again what I said went, because I was her twin. Bedsides, Rory never did get over the time Father Matthew tripped during Holy Communion and dropped a host at Uncle Connor's funeral.

'Tis a strange thing being an identical twin. People never do stop harking on about it. "You can't tell one from the other," they'd laugh. "There's something about the eyes," they'd say, "Caithlin's eyes are more wide open." I'd have had that one all my life if Caithlin hadn't developed the breathing problems in her final years. There was no need to look the eyes then. There was only ever the two of us. Caithlin was the first born and I came along twenty minutes later but it always WAS about Caithlin. Ma never had eyes for me.

My godmother's daughter sent condolences from Wicklow, enclosing a holy picture and a photo of my sister, that summer we spent near the beach at Bray. "Caithlin - sweet Star of the Sea. Shattered shells and strangled seaweed on the shore," she'd scribbled on the back. Mary always did fancy herself as a bit of a poet! "A lyricist amongst a nation of wordsmiths," was the way Da used to put it.

You could tell Da would've liked it if we'd been better at our studies. I was never one for reading – it made my eyes hurt but Caithlin'd sit on Da's lap and he'd turn the pages of her storybooks for her, whilst I'd sidle off into the pantry to try and cadge a slice of barm brack, spread with butter, off Ma."Get 'way outta that!" she'd more than likely say. Then Da'd tap his pipe and speak of Deidre of the Sorrows, whose beauty could only bring ruin to the realm of

Ireland, and Etaine whose name meant jealousy and who was turned into a pool of water.

At the convent, Mother Cecilia said we'd to be split up. The nuns mistrusted friendship. Caithlin was put on the top table for reading. My first confession was a fright – the heavy oak door swinging to, the pitch black, the cold hard seat, whispering how once I'd given dolly a bath in the holy water font above my bed, (Caithlin'd said 'twas a mortal sin so I'd go to hell,) the disgrace of wetting my pants…. Later, Ma'd demanded an explanation. My twin didn't waste time. 'Twas the Catholic way, you see: the truth above all else, never mind me getting belting.

Caithlin bagged Theresa as her confirmation name. Ma said I'd to have Clare. I said 'twasn't fair but Da said 'twas a grand name and didn't't Saint Clare follow the teachings of St. Francis in giving away all her worldly riches. But, the other girls laughed and called me "Poor Clare!"

When boys took an interest it was Caithlin who had the eyes wide open so she had her pick: Martin Lynch with the gacky-looking plimsolls and Declan Reidy who tried to woo her sporting a plaster cast. He'd broken his arm pegging it across the rec. in the rain (and Paddy Flynn laughing his cacks off all the while!) "And what'd I be wanting with a one-armed man? You'll no be dropping the hand!" cackled Caithlin, for she could be coarse like that.

All good boys from the Jesuit College who weren't't after any malarkey but Sister Aloysius warned we'd to be dog wide and said we'd not to talk to them. "Jaysus," declared my sister, "half the girls've got brothers at the school and 'tisn't as if they're non-Catholics!" So, once outside the school gates, she'd stuff her white gloves into her satchel and comb her long chestnut-brown hair in the street, (which Bernadette Maguire reckoned was common.)

I always wanted to strike out, wear a different outfit but Caithlin insisted we dress the same. Somehow she managed to look better. We never did marry - there was always the other twin in the way.

I went up to the presbytery on my own. The statue of The Sacred Heart gazed down on me. "Sorry for your troubles, you'll be wanting a cup of tea," murmured Sister Margaret, gliding silently out, in that way that nuns are taught to do. Father O'Rourke flicked nervously through the pages of his missal. "I'd a woman in earlier wanted a Latin mass," he confided, “said I could do it in Gaelic.” I wasn’t sure if he was joking but it didn’t seem to be the thing to be saying. I too missed the old certainties. I was glad when Sister Margaret slid back in. I’ve settled on “St. Patrick’s Breastplate” and “All Things Bright and Beautiful”,” I announced. “Very apposite,” declaimed Father O’Rourke. I wasn’t clear on his meaning but he was smiling faintly so I guessed, as my priest, he approved.

Well, I’ve arranged it all down to the last detail: bridge rolls, doilies, the car, Mass cards, rosaries to thank the altar boys, fifty pounds to the organist, lilies from me and Ave Maria as the coffin disappears.

Father O’Rouke’s calling it a merciful release. She got so weak, you see, but she was determined to stay at home with me until the end. Doctor Gavigan had shown me how to switch the oxygen on and off. ’Twasn’t difficult once I’d made my mind up. I was surprised really. But her eyes were wide open until the end.

THE LAST CHANCE SALOON
D. Warrington

Outside, it's wet, it's cold and it's windy. Shadows lurk in the doorways. But inside, the cards are rampant. One-eyed Jacks and smiling Queens run the court, fat Kings curse Ducks, and the steelworker with a wife and two kids to support, and he hasn't paid his rent yet, goes home broke…and the Doc, smelling of liniment oil still reminds me of a playful priest on the brink of madness.

It's a typical night in Bernie's back-street card room: a world loaded with compromise, corruption, and double cross, but with one exception - Dragon's beware, Selina's back in town: Selina with the chic smile and body worth staying up late for. She's straddling a beer crate next to her boyfriend: her boyfriend with the seducer's moustache and gaze of a lover who, on a cold morning, might jilt - but he hasn't and for twenty-odd years they've been shacked up together: Shame that. She still hurries lust.

I met her by chance on a wet afternoon in Brighton, and the pier fizzed. She was over-my-head, and under-my-chin - she was everywhere. She was the face in the dreams of soldiers, a kind of noir goddess you could only watch in a state of fever. The breeze on the promenade, wild with seagulls' cries, was never so salty.

And oh, what a time we had, and even though images often speak more eloquently than words, I felt like a chandelier out on the town - even the soles of my shoes glowed! We wined and dined, laughed and joked, watched films with sad endings, discussed Marx. And was a sunset ever more beautiful without her?

But that was a long time ago, times change - they always do. Possessing that magical 'it' - 'it' being the promise of sex, and blessed with nipples that pouted as if to say, 'get a load of this,' and hips that rolled with oceanic madness, she became a rare mixture of the unbridled and the very restrained. But fate will always be a passenger - it always is. When the gloss wore off she didn't just leave, she ran! But that was then, and this is now.

I shuffle the cards and ruffle the Aces: poker is a medium with no soul which relies on nerves of steel – but does it? Her boyfriend smiles and I hate him, I loathe him. He reminds me of a back street doctor who's got the abortion right, and when Jimmy-the-Greek and Charlie–the-feet both fold, he senses I'm bluffing. But am I? The question is, is he?

The turn of a card later, black eights stare back at me and I get the impression he'd marked the deck as he bets heavy – but does he have three? I don't know. But it doesn't matter I still got him beat - he's chasing rainbows. And then a strange thing happens, I glance at Selina with quiet concern, and feel myself crumbling. I feel the hurt she gave me receptive to the scent of forgiveness and embers of treachery, including revenge, fade in the wind, and perhaps his threadbare suit is a sure sign he's down on his luck and for the sake of Selina, and even though I'm shadowboxing with my soul, I let bygones be bygones...and let him win.

But do I?

The seductive walk, the heavily-lidded eyes, the inviting lips, that sensual face framed in a cascade of black hair, and even though her eyes are laced with melancholy, redemption in hell does not come easy, or cheap; naïveté is a mug's game. Chloroform poured on a rag and saying when is not beyond me. I've become an enemy to mankind – the perfect misanthropist, and perhaps now is my chance to get even.

But do I?

I glance at my cards, and then at her boyfriend, and he's not so smug. He's become a prim lion who lacks confidence: the twitching fingers and look-away smile are a dead giveaway. If hell is a mountain of fire, he's burning in the Alps, and I've seen it before a thousand times: long nights in the company of demons have its rewards. Hannibal Lecter told me!

"Well?" says Bernie, looking at me. "Is he bluffing? Are you gonna call or raise him?"

And I'm lost for words; I can't think straight, my mind just won't function. I'm dancing with devils and sleeping with monsters. Disaster's cunning knows no bounds, and if I'm not careful I could end up in a care home! Life has become nothing more than a kaleidoscope of shattered illusions.

But is it?

Selina once told me 'The most prolific weapon in a lady's armoury is a man's imagination,' and she was right, except…? Grandeur's decline is well past its infancy. Some things are meant to be - they always are.

"Well?" says Bernie yet again. "What's it to be, call, raise, or fold?"

...and the tension is becoming unbearable - I'm walking a cellophane bridge. You can think one thing and do another.

"Raise," says Charlie. "Never give a sucker an even break!"

"Fold," yells the Doc. "He's got the nuts."

"Call," screams Jimmy. "He's bluffing,"...and Selina still looks utterly divine.

But is she?

My thoughts are my own and no one can steal them. Beneath that guarded look of hers, I sense she's praying I'll fold. She knows I've got her boyfriend beat and she's begging me for forgiveness.

"For the last time," says Bernie. "What's it to be?"

Outside, it's stopped raining. A chill November wind blows through the alleyways, neon street lighting pales in the early morning sky, and someone's left a television set on in the Radio Rental shop opposite, but not the sound; breakfast TV is showing; Richard and Judy strutting their stuff...and a man going to work comes down the street with his sandwiches tucked under his arm, sandwiches his wife made – oh lucky man.

…and I feel like a lush pillow just made love on – but without the lace.

Third Prize

Matthew Preston was born in Coventry and attended Nottingham Trent University. Fleeing expectations of a 'real job', he spent two years in China, teaching. Following travelling and acquiring a PGCE he taught in Germany and met the woman who became his wife and mother to his twins.

He now teaches at a Primary School in Leicester and has had short stories published by Pewter Rose Press and Sixth Element Publishing. Now he just needs to finish his novel!

PRACTICAL PARENTING

Matthew Preston

DAY 1

"Oh shit!" James uttered out loud the words that had flooded his brain. "Shit!"

In his arms was a baby, not any old baby, his baby!

"There you are! A healthy, baby boy."

It was not that this new baby son was a surprise; it was more the fact that he suddenly felt a great weight of pressure, figuratively speaking, weighing on him.

"This isn't real..."

"Your son appears healthy so we'll have you and your wife back home shortly." The doctor or nurse, James had forgotten, breezed out leaving him holding the baby, literally this time.

The small sleeping infant was perfect and despite himself he felt a rush of love towards his son, a tear appeared at the corner of his eye.

The next few hours were a trial of screaming, crying and hideous smelling nappies. The night was sleepless but the morning was an awakening of very different kind.

DAY 2

Olly (the name that James and his wife had chosen for their new son) tottered into their room and climbed into bed, shuffling in the middle of his two sleeping parents.

It took James and his wife Sarah a couple of seconds to realise whom this little body belonged. Olly was now 4 years old, a vast change since the newborn of only a few hours earlier.

"He's getting big!" remarked a drowsy James.

"Well, they do say that children grow up fast," an equally sleepy Sarah replied.

The couple during that day became acutely aware that their son was growing up very fast before their eyes.

Tantrums, playing in mud playing the computer, Olly did them all. His language as it should have been was that of a child approaching eight years old as was his intelligence and, his appearance.

His parents were not unduly concerned at this rapid increase in maturity only of the severity of the financial constraints it might put upon them. That, and James just could not figure where Olly was getting all his energy from. The football, the running, jumping, screaming, bouncing, shouting... James felt his head might explode if this carried on. He looked over at Sarah; she appeared much calmer than he was. He secretly hoped she was just as lost as he was deep down.

DAY 3

Another morning, another surge of growth and as this was a Monday it was time for their son to start his schooling, he was intelligent and he was now a nine year old, if they did not make a decision soon he would be at secondary school by the time they did. Fortunately they had places booked for both the local schools this week.

James and Sarah took Olly to school, his first and only day of Primary School, They took their excited son to the school gates. He kissed his mum on the cheek waved at his dad before walking through the school gates.

The pair ambled home and sat on the sofa with synchronised sighs. This was the first time they had been able to sit down in three days. The desolation of having a child had obviously been of a great effect to both parents and house, which looked like it had been both burgled and bombed.

DAY 4

The teenage years hit like a hurricane with grunting, shouting and the slamming of doors. How James wished for the relative ease of when Olly had been a baby.

They struggled to contain the more reckless aspects of his nature, the underage drinking and the sex (James had a sneaking admiration for his son after inadvertently witnessing indiscreet liaisons with 3 separate girls).

The day felt like it lasted a year.

That evening however, they sat around the dinner table for what they all knew would be the last time. A meal of chicken nuggets and chips (today's favourite) passed in silence.

Olly raced up to his room but whether he stayed there the night his parents did not know. James and Sarah settled down on their sofa with a bottle of wine and a glass each. The mood was grim.

"Well, we only have one more day!" James said with a sigh.

"It's been harder than I thought," agreed Sarah. "But I really love him...can't we keep him?"

"You know they won't let us do that, besides he's too big now, we'll just have to do it properly..."

DAY 5

Olly had a lie-in. When he arrived downstairs, mid-morning, he appeared to have miraculously matured; he was polite, well mannered and helpful.

This caught his parents off guard.

They made the most of their last day together catching a film; going into the town and laughing more than they had ever laughed.

At 8pm they received the knock on the door they had been dreading, today more than any other day. At the door were a retrieval team from Mayfly Ltd.

Sarah opened the door.

"Good evening madam, we are here to retrieve unit 53684," the team leader said consulting his clipboard, "Is it ready for collection?"

James had arrived at Sarah's shoulder; he turned and yelled back into the house, "Olly, it's for you!"

Olly trudged up to the door "Love you mum!" he said hugging Sarah, "and you pops!" he said as his dad squeezed his shoulder. He was led to the waiting unmarked black van.

"If you could just sign here and print your name..." prompted the team leader. "Okay, here's your parenting licence, you are already to have kids of your own now. It seems healthy enough! Please fill out this customer satisfaction card and tell us how well the unit did, what you say really matters to us!"

He handed over the certificate and form and jumped into the passenger seat of the van.

The van left, and James and Sarah could just make out the face of Olly in the back window.

"Fancy going upstairs then?" asked James, hopefully.

WAITING
Sarah-Jane Blake

It's 7.30pm and I'm waiting for the phone to ring once, and cut off. That's the signal he gives me when I should head out to meet him.

It's cold out tonight. I should be curling up on the sofa for the evening instead of hiding out in a dark corner of a deserted park for half an hour. It's been four days since I saw him last though and even if I back out tonight, I've no way of letting him know. Never call back. That is the one rule I must abide by.

It's 8pm and I'm still waiting. I waste some time by preparing for my exit. I need to get out of here as quickly as possible when the signal comes. I would bring the car round to save even more time, but I can't risk being away from the phone in case I miss the call and no matter how reluctant I am to venture out tonight, I cannot miss that call.

I spend so much time waiting. I can't help but wonder how I let my life come to this, why I let my life come to this. From the moment I first met him, I knew that there was a danger that I would become addicted. I heard the alarm bells, saw all of the warning signs and chose to ignore them. But even if I'd had a glimpse of what my future was to become, I'm not sure I'd have acted any differently.

It's 8.30pm and I pick up the phone to make sure that there is a dial tone. Immediately I regret it, what if he tried to give the signal at the exact time that I picked up the handset? I'm anxious now, angry and impatient. The child in me wants to spite him but what can I do? Not turn up? He knows that I'll go running. He knows beyond all doubt that he is the one in control of our arrangement.

I managed to hide my addiction from my family for several months until the lying and sneaking around became too much for me to bear. I broke down and told my mum the truth one afternoon, after she overheard me plotting to get my next fix. My family are trying desperately hard to be supportive, but I can see the disappointment in their eyes.

It's 9pm now and I am pacing the room like a caged animal, my rage building. My mind is spinning with negativity. He has always called by now. He's not going to make it, is he? I've been sat here waiting all this time for nothing. I could have made dinner or watched a movie, even gone to bed, anything but sitting here, waiting. I can't believe he's doing this to me, fucking selfish bastard. My anger rises by the second, like mercury shooting up the glass vial of a thermometer. I'm not ready to concede defeat yet though.

I need a distraction, something to calm me down and occupy my mind to make the waiting less infuriating. I decide that if the signal doesn't come by 10pm, then that's it, I'll accept that tonight I'll be left wanting. I flick mindlessly through the television channels, but nothing catches my attention. I switch on my games console and start to play a game but I can't concentrate and find myself getting even more frustrated. This is ridiculous. When did I become so pathetically dependant?

It's 9.30pm and the phone rings, but it's not him. I stare at the phone, torn between not wanting to ignore the caller and not wanting to tie up the line. Eventually the caller hangs up and I clear the missed call from the handset display.

I sigh and wander over to the window, trying to keep my breathing even to calm my jangling nerves. There is no life to be seen outside, rain has fallen heavily and the roads are glistening under the dull light of the street lamps. It's so cold that it won't be long before the damp roads start to freeze, so I throw my black hat and gloves on to the pile of things that I've gathered together for our meeting. It's better if I am less recognizable anyway. Safer.

It's 9.55pm when it happens. My patience (worn thin though it is) has finally been rewarded. The phone rings once and stops, his number flashing briefly on the handset display. My heart is pounding as I pull on my outdoor clothing, snatch up the car keys and run out of the house.

My destination is a short ten minute drive away and I can't stop smiling. I turn the stereo up loud and start singing along as I race through the deserted streets. My anger and impatience melt away as the sense of sheer relief courses through my veins. Tonight I'll get my fix. Tonight I'll be able to sleep peacefully.

Finally reaching the side street that leads to the park I slow the car and pull up as close to the entrance as I can, and then I wait. It is not long before I can see his silhouette in the distance. I strain my eyes against the dark night to make sure that there is nobody else around.

He reaches the place where I have pulled over and passes me without acknowledgement before walking towards the darkest corner of the park. I wait until he is out of sight before stepping out of the car and into the freezing night to follow him.

I never intended to become a mistress. Does anyone actually plan that sort of thing? Love is the most irresistible of drugs, and despite the pain of the addiction, I seek out hit after hit in the hope that one day he will provide the constant supply that I crave and leave his whole life to be with me.

It's been ten years since we met.

I'm still waiting.

THE LAST CONFESSION

S.M. Nelson

I am not afraid, yet my fingers tremble. I try to stiffen them into obedience, clenching my fists until my bitten nails make red crescents in my palm. I didn't think it would end this way. I never thought I would be able to pinpoint the end of my life, the beginning of my descent. But it won't be long now; half an hour, perhaps an hour at most. I close my eyes for a few moments, but still I see her. She looks at me with her dead eyes, dead eyes that cannot see. She is blind to me, yet I can feel her eyes burning me, her blank stare slowly ripping me apart.

It didn't have to be this way, I know that. Mr Hawkins told me he could get me off; he could spare me this end. Martha, he said in that grating voice of his, Martha, listen to me. You did not mean to do this; you did not mean to hurt her. Let me help you. But he could never understand me, and so he could never help me. He didn't care whether I had done it or not. I don't blame him for that, but I wish he had listened to me. He only asked me about it once, the first time we met.

It was late one afternoon, and although my window was too small to let much light in, I could see that behind the bars the sky was mauve and heavy. He walked in apprehensively, clutching his hat in one large, ham-like hand. I could see his knuckles straining hard against the taut skin of his fist. His eyes met mine and darted away immediately, flicking around the stark room. After a moment he looked back at me, a smile twisting his thin mouth.

Martha, he said, I am Mr Hawkins. I am going to act on your defence, so I need you to trust me, do you understand? I looked at him for a while, feeling a bizarre pleasure in his discomfort. I knew I could never trust him. I understand, I said. Would you like to hear what happened? His Adam's apple bobbed in his throat as he swallowed, and he perched uncertainly on the chair opposite mine. He cleared his throat as he did so, and I took that as a sign to begin.

I didn't plan to do it. I hope you know that, sir. I am not a monster, like they say. I am not evil. But I will not lie; I did do it. It was the second day of June, and I was in the garden. I was kneeling in the soil, my fingers scrambling in the dirt. I could feel tiny grains of earth under my nails, and it made me angry. I do not like being unclean. My apron was soiled too, even though I had tied it up at the top. I would have to bleach it to get the stains out, and even then it would not be as white as before. It was hot and I felt uncomfortable, but I kept fumbling in the soil, pulling the potatoes out one by one and placing them in the heavy metal bucket beside me.

I wanted Mr Carson to enjoy his supper that night. He had been away for a week on business, and would be back that eve. I hoped he had brought me something. Last time he brought me back a dress. I had never seen anything so beautiful; it was a taffeta dress, white with daisies. I could not wear it outside, for the neighbours would talk, but I had often worn it in secret inside the house. I walked the length of the hallways and pretended I was lady of the house, my shoes tapping on the polished floors, the skirt rustling as I walked.

I filled the pail up with the potatoes and lifted it, jutting it above my hip as I walked to the house. I could see Mrs Carson from the parlour window, watching me. She always watched me. I did not think she knew, but perhaps she suspected. I went into the kitchen, making sure my eyes did not reach hers. I emptied the pail over the sink and shook the potatoes out. They tumbled over each other, crumbs of soil flecking over the porcelain. I felt another flicker of annoyance as the perfect whiteness was marked with filth.

I bent over and picked up the few spuds that had fallen to the floor, and then I saw her. She was standing in the doorway, her mouth in a tight line. Can I get you anything, ma'am, I said. She was silent. I turned back to the sink, but then she spoke. Who got you that dress, Martha, she said. Who got you that dress? You will answer me immediately.

I looked at her and saw tears in her eyes. I watched as they pooled, gathering behind her eyes, then spilling over her smooth cheeks. I cleared my throat. I bought the dress myself, ma'am, I said. I bought it with my wages. Mrs Carson stamped her foot. We do not pay you enough for that, Martha, she hissed. You are lying! I said nothing, looking at the delicate pearl choker around her plump neck. She took a step forward, her chin wobbling like a petulant child's. You will leave this house at once, she said. Collect your belongings and leave. Now!

I looked at the floor, praying for Mr Carson to return. But the doorway remained empty, and I felt her fingers close over my wrists. Martha, she shouted, her voice cracking at the 'r' in my name, Martha you will leave! I turned my back and walked slowly over to the sink, picking up the bucket as though she'd never spoken. I could not go, sir, because my master loved me. When he arrived he would shun his wife and pull me into his arms, showering me with gifts and kisses. I closed my eyes tightly, praying that any minute he would come storming into the kitchen and tell his wife the truth. But still he did not come.

My neck jolted back sharply, and I let out a cry as I struggled to turn around. Mrs Carson had grabbed hold of the thick braid of hair that hung down my back and was shrieking like a madwoman. Get out of my house, she screamed, get out! Her fingernails clawed at my face, and I strained to push her away. I remember thinking how strong she was. She was stronger than I expected, and though I tried to push her away I could not. My fingers were still curled around the handle of the bucket and I swung it upwards. It hit her in the face and she screamed again, letting go of my hair. She clutched one hand to her bruised face, the other still scrabbling for my face. I swung the bucket again, bringing it down this time. It hit her head hard and silently. Perhaps it did make a sound really, sir, but I cannot remember one. I brought it down again and again over her head until she was slumped on the floor, her face resting against the warm kitchen tiles. I placed the bucket carefully beside and then waited for her to move.

I'm not sure how long it was before I turned her over. They say it was hours, but I cannot imagine I would have just stood there for so long. But perhaps I did, for the next thing I remember was the sound of Mr Carson's carriage clattering down the drive. It was dark, yet I could clearly make out my mistress, still lying obediently on the floor. I stooped over her and slid my fingers under her shoulders. I remember that my hands did not shake. I turned her over and placed her on her back. Her eyes were open, and they stared up at me accusingly. I see those eyes everywhere now, sir, even when I close my own. I looked at the crooked shape she made on the floor, a dark pool of blood neatly encircling her head, seeping into the fissures in the tiles, and making a mess of my nice clean floor.

I could hear Mr Carson's footsteps approaching, so I quickly stepped over his wife and began flinging the potatoes back into the bucket. They bounced over each other, hitting the walls of the bucket and making a satisfying pinging noise. I knew when Mr Carson had entered the kitchen because that was when all the shouting began. I cannot remember what he was saying to me, but I kept a calm head in the situation, the way a good maid always should. Supper will be ready soon sir, I told him. I'm making your favourite meal. Please calm yourself, sir. Don't fret about the mess on the floor, it will wash out, I assure you. Please sir, calm yourself. Please sir. Please calm down.

And so that is what I told Mr Hawkins, and that is what happened. He was quiet for a very long while afterward. His tongue darted over his lips, moistening them, as though listening to my story had fatigued him in the worst possible way. He said, I do not think this was your fault, Martha. Your mind does not work the way it should, you did not know what you were doing. I laughed at that. I knew what he wanted me to say, but the asylum did not appeal to me. And that is why I have chosen this end.

Two men come into my room, and grip me firmly by each arm. I do not struggle, as they expect me to. I have nothing to struggle for. They lead me down the dark corridors and into the large room. I see the thick rope hanging there patiently, the noose swinging slightly with expectance. I am not afraid, yet my fingers tremble.

NOT HERMAN
Jon Dix

'Call me Ishmael.'

The Grocer looked up in surprise at hearing those familiar opening words; he wondered why the Mod was quoting 'Moby Dick' to him. He turned down the radio on Harold Wilson's speech and stared curiously at the Mod.

'I beg your pardon?' and he waited for the Mod to repeat the phrase. But the Mod didn't repeat it. Instead the Mod said 'Caught me fish tail!' and turned around and showed the white stuffing leaking from a tear in the bottom of his faded green parka.

'I done it jumping some railings.'

'Oh I see, that's quite a rip, how can I help?'

'You got needle and fred, like in them travel sewing kits?'

'Yes…um… I think they're over there on the

rack… with elastic and travel games… near the bottom… above the magnetic chess'

He watched the Mod poke about on the rack, and return to the counter with a 'handy pack' of assorted needles, safety pins and different coloured threads wound round flat waxed card. The Grocer assessed the tall chubby youth, and noted the pork pie hat squeezed onto his pork pie head. The Mod looked pleased and placed the sewing kit on the counter.

'This packs got the most 'greens' in it, see?' he held the packet to his parka sleeve and admired the colour match.

'Yes lovely, I hope you can sew?' he said to the Mod, smiling.

'Nah, but me bird's outside, she can sew,' and he gave a backward nod toward the door.

The Grocer dropped the sewing kit in a brown paper bag and gave the bag a cheerful twist as only grocers can.

'Are you enjoying Brighton?' asked the Grocer.

The Mod shrugged.

'It's alright I spose... Prefer Margate meself.'

'I thought you said "Call me Ishmael" when you came in.' The Grocer gave a half laugh along with his attempt let the Mod in on his amusing highlight of the day.

'What?' The Mod looked confused,

'I said… I thought you said *Call me Ishmael* when you actually said *Caught-me-fish-tail.*' The Grocer explained. The Mod stared at the Grocer suspiciously and said nothing. There was an uncomfortable pause.

'You know...Moby Dick...' added the Grocer hopeful of some comprehension by the Mod.

'What? What you talkin' about?' the Mod gave a wary look to the Grocer.

'Nothing, er, never mind. That's ten pence ha'penny please.'

The Mod dumped a sandy handful of assorted bronze on the glass counter and mumbled something about 'daylight robbery'. He waited as the Grocer counted it, blew off the sand and slid an overpaid ha'penny back across the scratched glass. The Mod sneered and said 'Keep the change' as if a ha'penny was a sizable donation. He snatched the paper bag and headed out. Just as he was closing the door, he leaned his fat pork pie head back in and shouted.

'Oi Ponce! Nuffin wrong with my dick mate,' then he slammed the door shut.

The Grocer sighed thoughtfully and imagined a great school of sperm whales eating Mods and Rockers from the beach later that day. Twenty whales, massed grey bodies half out from the surf. Their battleship coloured heads – vast as London buses - cocked sideways, lurching in arcs, scything through the sand and bodies, ordered rank and column of ivory teeth snapping at disordered parkas and leathers.

He dreamed of the boys flopping and flailing, clamped by determined long jaws as the whales threshed and bucked backwards into the cold red waves. 'Rude Boys' and 'Rockers' dangling from the whale's indifferent smiles like sardines from puffin beaks.

He pictured the boys being dragged screaming into the sea, to be carried down to the squid-ink deep in open mouthed silence. Fans of 'Pirate ship radio' hauled below to where the wrecks of *real* pirate ships lay.

He imagined the boys in the crushing cold of the fathomless dark water. Their faces frozen wide eyed with shock. He could clearly see the boys in his mind, bearing their mute screams with all the ear-splitting hush of Munch's painting.

This wasn't an idle thought in the Grocer's mind; it was more of an over-optimistic prayer. He smiled, turned the volume up on Mr Wilson's speech and went back to unpacking a gross of sherbet dib dabs.

FIRST TASTE

Tony Gott

"Go on! Drink it!" they cried. I looked at the tiny shot glass, but did not move. I knew that there was only a tiny amount of the pale golden liquid inside it. I knew that I could swallow it all in one draught, but that was not what my friends wanted. They expected me to savour the taste, to delight as it seared my tongue with its burning harshness.

Nervously I turned the glass round in my fingers, feeling the cold smooth surface beneath the roughness of my fingertips. As the glass moved some of the whisky inside sloshed up the side of the glass. It slowly crept back – thick and viscous as syrup, leaving a lustrous residue coating the surface.

I looked up, trying to delay the inevitable. My friends' expectant faces all looked back at me, glistening with sweat due to the roaring fire in the corner of the bar. I shuffled my feet on the uneven bare wooden floorboards, feeling them moan and creak beneath my feet like some discordant old piano.

"Must I..." I began to ask, but their resounding "yes!" interrupted me. I pulled up all my reserve, and without any further pause I knew that I must act. I drained the glass, feeling the whisky pour into my mouth.

I could not detect any of the flavours that I had been told to expect. No notes of heather or scents of oak caskets. What I did find was a burning torrent sliding down my throat. Even as I swallowed I felt it move down my gullet like a ball of molten lead. I felt as if my lungs would burst, my eyes were watering, my face was flushed and I coughed and spluttered.

The faces of my friends were an audience eager to her my judgement on my first drink of whisky. "Well…" I paused, unsure what to say. "You'll have another won't you?" one of them asked. "Make a real man of you."

My mouth seemed to move of its own volition. "Just one more," I said.

Second Prize

Tom Bannister is an Essex-native who has divided his last six years up fairly between China and the UK. He wrote this story whilst completing his doctoral research in Chengdu, one of the fastest growing cities in the world. It is a bike ride he makes every week.

WRITING WITH WATER: A Short Cycle Ride through a Chinese City

Tom Bannister

Head swimming a languid back-stroke after a lunchtime beer, I emerge from the blacks and blues of the lift-shaft into the yellows and whites of the late afternoon. Feet on grimy, rusting aluminium, I push away, nodding to the dozing gate-guard as I breeze slowly past. As the sun beats a pounding tattoo onto the crumbling asphalt, I steer the bike with my thighs, fingers tracing esoteric patterns across a shiny screen. On the side of the lane a frail old man practises calligraphy on the pavement with a goat-hair brush and a pot of water. I ignore him as I glide past, his first characters already evaporating into the ether as he continues to write his ephemeral prose. Playlist on shuffle and floating towards the heat-haze, I reach up and place the headphones into my ears.

I accelerate around the corner, the thud of my steadily pounding feet matching the hurrying beat of the indie music. The suggestion of a passing dumpling shop wafts under my nose, sounding like Manchester but smelling like China. I sail past becalmed motorised rickshaws and women hauling baskets of sand on their bowed backs, easily the fastest presence on the slumbering back-lane. As a guitar solo echoes off the flaking whitewash of communist work-units I glide serenely across a junction, confidently ignoring the speculative red light. I pass a construction site where migrant labourers lie dreaming of rice paddies against the Ginkgo trees that line the street, their crumpled postures framed by the towering cranes behind them. As the landscape dissolves around me into a crescendo of blurred leaves and guitar arpeggios I hit a pot-hole, the shock-waves jarring my bones and shaking the sweat from my forehead. The street ahead returns to focus and I see a junction rapidly approaching. I apply my bike's worn-out brakes as the murmur of a Warrington drawl fades into the urban miasma around me.

I face the torrent of traffic alongside a stripe of people assembled into a fleeting moment of intransience by tides of fate and circumstance. As one drum beat fuses into another, the eyes alongside me coalesce into the hollow stare of the collectively bored. I push off before the cars on either side of me have come to a halt, parting the sea of red, black and silver as I glide into the cycle-lane. As the beats layer onto one another, dancing their way across the roofs of the rapidly rising ranks of buildings, I change gear. Suddenly the music explodes into a chaos of electronica and I pedal faster, swooping down and around an overloaded bus. As my wheels fly across the hot tarmac, I weave a lazy pattern into the meandering traffic, signing my brief existence into the heavy air with a flourish of balding rubber and oxidising metal. With an emerald light slowly turning to ruby ahead of me, I speed up rather than slow down, the beat driving me forward and across the teeming intersection.

As the buildings rear-up around me, enclosing the tree-lined road in a canyon of glass and scaffolding, the music comes to an abrupt halt. I slide silently through the rapidly coagulating traffic, my headphones blocking out the sound of angry horns and my lips sealed against the acidic fumes. The music begins again, the soft trickle of a folk song washing over me in a gentle mist of female harmonics and lightly picked guitars. In the ether of exhaust fumes the limp leaves of the urban poplar trees dissolve into the dancing silvery tips of willows whispering their way into the breeze of an English summer afternoon. The stationary cars around me are hedgerows, the towering buildings are oaks and ashes and the reds and browns of the workers scampering across the bamboo scaffolding are the reds of wrens and the browns of thrushes. As the pitch of the folk singer's voice starts to resonate with the urban hum around me, the road spills around the city's public square.

Mao looks straight at me, accusing finger pointing to the sky, as the corn and barley voice in my ear merges into the conch shell clattering of an early 60's ska beat. His eyes follow me as I glide around the yawning plaza, getting ever closer to his looming presence. As the horn section rasps out a celebration of independence from a dying empire I keep my eyes on his colossal feet standing in their wild graffiti of potted orchids. Suddenly I am on his side of the square and as I pass under his massive outstretched arm I can't help but look up and into his stony concrete eyes. And yet he is looking away, glaring at the hundreds of tourists clicking and clucking in the square in front of him. As the sun sets into a smoggy cloud behind of me and the neon lights are brought to life in front of me, Mao stands, feet wide apart, in a bed of orchids swaying softly to the walking bass-line.

The warm air breathes its dirt and dust onto my sweating brow as I head away from Mao's square and into the neon evening, the beat changing from a breezy African folk, to a thundering dub-step, and onwards into a dirty three-chord punk. The stagnant air crackles and clicks around me as I float past tired shoppers emerging in their shiny new cars from cavernous car-parks. I swim through the humid night, away from this iridescent atoll and back into the swarming back streets, the crowded restaurants steaming with soy-sauce and shimmering with the ghosts of red lanterns. Up ahead a bottleneck of cars heading into a dark tunnel signals that my brief foray into speed will come to an end, and yet I continue to overtake. Heading towards the sound and fury of the approaching storm, each bolt the flickering syllable of a brief candle, my fingers tap on the rusting break levers to the quickening beat of the future.

THE RECYCLING OPERATIVE

Rebekah Hardy

The cat had been quite large and sleek of coat in life. Now it lay in the road looking small, crusty and definitely dead.

Sad, thought Big Dave, as he noticed the little corpse in the road. "Aw, someone has hit the cat," he rumbled, leaving the wheelie bin he was trundling.

"Oi! Big Dave! Wha's up? Stop slacking!" Little D's thin, reedy voice erupted from the recycling lorry.

"Come on, Knucklehead!" Little D sighed and glanced down the street. Nice, thought Little D, nice houses, nice gardens, very nice cars. A worm of jealousy flicked its tail in Little D's head.

Big Dave rarely noticed the roads, streets and lanes his job took him down. He felt no resentment at the surrounding affluence. He just looked down at the dead cat, as if some sadness resonated deep within him.

"The lady at the big house has got cats." The sentence was constructed with care. "I will see if this is one of hers."

And with this thought securely in place, Big Dave carefully scooped up the corpse. He purposefully ignored the swearing and thumping of the steering wheel from the cab.

Little D joined Big Dave at the door.

"How do you know she has cats?"

"Cat food tins. Lots!"

"Ooh, Sherlock Holmes ain't ya just! Well if it's a lady with cats, you can bet that the house'll stink of cats. And she'll be old and have a hairy cardy on and fingerless gloves. Bet ya!"

"You've killed George!" The lady, tall, slender and graceful, swayed at the impact of the scene before her.

"Nah, we didn't do it. Big Dave found it in the road. It's yours then?" Turn up for the books, Little D thought, blonde, blue eyed, more Swedish au pair than cardy-clad granny.

"Yes, Yes, I hadn't even noticed he had gone out." Tears began to prickle in her eyes.

"Have you got a box or something? Only me and Knucklehead'll have to get back to the bins."

"Sorry, yes, yes, I'll get one. I was going to put it out for recycling..."

"Here. Thank you, put him in. I'll bury him in his favourite…" At this the tears overwhelmed her and the cat lady sobbed as Big Dave put George into his cardboard coffin.

Big Dave took a deep breath and as he handed the box to the cat lady said,

"Can death be sleep, when life is but a dream,
And senses of bliss pass as a phantom by?
The transient pleasures as a visitor seem,
And yet we think the greatest pains to die."

The lady cried some more at that and thanking, Big Dave and Little D, took George to his final resting place. Dave went back to his wheelie bin, normality flooding back into the space where the cat had been.

"Oi! Knucklehead! Where'd you learn that spouty stuff?"

"Dat was Keats. Me Mam gave me a book."

"Didn't even know you could read!" said Davina, nearly under her breath.

RESCUED AT MIDNIGHT

Megan Flowers

Alina sat in her Victorian style cottage nestling a coffee by an open fire. The different flame shades fought each other as they bit away at the wooden logs she had cut down two weeks previous. She curled up into a ball oblivious to the howling wind rattling her windows. Her thoughts had drifted off to her husband, Evan. He had been missing for three everlasting years. She allowed herself a single tear to create a river down her cheek at the thought of him. She yearned for his tender touch to caress her cheek as her thoughts were greedy in want for him. She wanted to brush her delicate hand through his blond curls and to drown thoughts in the oceanic pools of his eyes.

The gust of air that had thrust open her window brought her out of her reverie. She jumped up allowing her coffee to escape over the rim of her mug. She rushed to the window forcing it shut with all the strength she managed to muster. She bolted it shut just like she had her heart. She collapsed onto the floor feeling out of place in her home.

A few minutes later she retrieved a cloth from the sink and drifted ghostly towards the stain on the pine wood flooring. She gently scrubbed the floor as she had her mind days after Evan disappeared. She brought herself up gracefully and headed back towards the sink. The water discoloured after she ran her cloth under it, a murky brown filled the sink. Her life had been dull for three years and she had brought it on herself. She had made herself alone when she blocked off her need for human contact.

As she glanced up she caught her lover's reflection in the window. The image had retrieved the words in her mouth and turned them into dust. Her emerald eyes flickered for a few seconds before she lifted a fragile hand up onto the window to touch him. She craved the softness of his peachy skin. As she reached the iciness of the window the wind stole him from her along with the only feeling she had in years. Alina slapped herself mentally before heading towards the bedroom they once shared.

She swapped her lemon coloured scoop neck maxi dress for a mid-length midnight blue silk nightdress. Minutes later she sat down at her dresser. She stared mindlessly into the mirror searching for answers she knew she wouldn't find. She shifted her focus to the music box she had received the Christmas before her life disappeared along with her love. She opened it slowly careful not to damage the fabric. She remembered the day Evan gave it to her, she had been standing by the raging fire, reminiscing all the memories they had shared together. He had dashed through the front door clutching the box at his thigh as though it carried treasure. He had it made and they were the couple dancing to the music as they had at their wedding.

Those memories were now filled with a void of nothing and the treasure she filled it with lay there collecting dust. She turned the box around to the back and fiddled with the key making the happy couple turn to the music. She smiled faintly at the recognition of the music but she didn't allow herself to think of their happy day. She felt guilty being happy without him, they were to be happy together. She left it running as she went to lay on the bed snuggling into the lilac satin which covered the pillow and quilt. She wrapped herself up like a parcel and sat in the centre of the feathered bed. She stared off into the living room waiting for the door to open as she had for the past years. Alina sometimes lost hope that he would come home but still she waited for him.

She was still sitting there when the doorknob rattled. She jumped and dived to the door and flung it open to be thrown back onto the floor with a gale of wind. Unfazed she jumped up and launched herself across the field in front of her cottage.

"Evan!" she screamed repeatedly. She stopped short of the cliff and dropped onto the clamminess of the grass. Her fall wasn't cushioned and she smacked her head on the rocks which had been thrown about like a rag doll by the gale.

"I don't want to be the meaning of my name, I don't want to be alone," she cried before closing her eyes. She lay there a few minutes before her heart started to pump faster than it had in years. She hadn't felt the sensation since Evan was gone. She forced open her lids and sat up in search for him. Before long she stared up into the radiance of the moon and started wishing. It came true; she could feel his arms around her waist hugging her to his cold muscular body. She rested her head back onto his shoulder and let out a sigh.

"You came back." She smiled with contempt and snuggled closer to him. She stared up into his eyes and noticed the change. She was dazed and couldn't bring herself to question why his eyes had turned a blood red. She felt complete at last after what felt like eternity. "Please don't leave me again," she begged mindlessly. He soothingly placed two fingers on her lips to quieten her. He closed her lids lightly and caressed her pale lips. "What's the time Evan?" She asked.

"Midnight, sweetheart," he replied. "And don't worry we'll be together for eternity, just sleep for now we'll talk when you awaken."

As she rest on his shoulder she felt him brush aside her chocolate curls and a tingling sensation occurred down her neck. She mumbled before she blackened wondering in what way had she been rescued at midnight.

HENRY WHO HATED CATS

Jan Collins

Once upon a time, Henry hated cats. Not any more, though. I don't mean to say that Henry underwent a conversion experience, that now he loves cats. It's just that, these days, he doesn't care.

Let me tell you the story. When I say that Henry hated cats, it would be more accurate to say that, in the first instance, Henry hated me. I was that cat. I never fathomed out what I did to incur his wrath. All it was, really, is that I used his ornamental flowerpot for a crafty pee on the way home for supper. If you've never done it in a flower pot, I recommend you try. The soil is soft and easy to dig. Your feet are clear of wet grass and hard tarmac. You are raised above the height of any passing predator, and can do your business in safety. A flowerpot is good. At first I only did this infrequently. But when I saw what an effect it had on Henry, I did it more and more. I would sit on the pot, facing into his lounge window; I would fix him with a hypnotic feline stare; I would raise my tail to maximum, like a regimental standard on the field of battle; and I would let fly. By the time Henry emerged, incandescent, into the garden, I would be three streets away and hardly breaking a sweat (if cats could sweat).

It became a daily pleasure, winding up Henry. Of course, he retaliated. At first there were the bits of orange peel placed in the pot. What good this was meant to do, heaven knows. The peel found its way swiftly on to the ground, along with the poo and half the contents of the pot. Next it was the pepper spray; and there I was, thinking that pepper sprays were illegal in this fine upstanding country of ours. Lastly, it was the offensive electrical whistling machine. Set to a frequency beyond the hearing of Henry, but for the maximum annoyance of us cats, this proved to be the hardest weapon to combat. But a swift spurt from a well-endowed tomcat, aimed at the battery, eventually disabled the machine for good.

Henry spent a fortnight arguing with the factory, believing it had malfunctioned of its own accord.

And so war was declared. It was something bigger than a neighbourly row between Henry and myself. I called in the troops. And this is the story of our first (and last) battle.

It was late evening. In the distance, a fox was barking. Nearer at hand, the sounds of day were giving way to the sounds of night, when all Henries are afraid and vulnerable, while we cats are in our element. A barn owl, ghostly pale, flew past in search of her prey. The wind soughed in the trees and rippled Henry's pond like a spirit passing over the face of the waters. Street lamps cast long shadows; between the lamps the world lay blacker than a starless sky. Nothing moved, nothing that could be detected. Windows were lit behind drawn curtains as Henries protected themselves against the alien darkness.

It was then that my followers and I gathered on his lawn. At first I howled, as only a cat or a troubled spirit can howl. Gradually, first one and then another joined in. The air was full of howling, wild but pregnant with meaning, musical but unlike any music made or heard before. We howled as if our lives depended on it. Our song was magnificent.

And of course Henry responded. He came out into the dark, angry in the extreme. His anger turned to fear as, in the darkness, he was met with many pairs of eyes, disembodied eyes, golden eyes, glowing with an energy which came from no earthly source, all focused on him. The music swelled. The darkness grew deeper, offset against those ghastly eyes. Henry was terrified.

Then, at a command from me, the music stopped. A terrifying moment of silence followed. And as one we spat at Henry. It was like a bomb exploding, like a whole crate of fireworks lit at once. We spat with all the venom of long-suppressed rage.

And it had its desired effect. Henry stopped, clutched at his chest, and fell heavily. He lay unmoving. I motioned to the rest and we approached the fallen Henry, surrounding him. His eyes, still open, registered terror. Then they closed, never to open again.

As Henry breathed his last, I stood beside his head, my mouth close to his ear. And I purred. God, did I purr. After all, no one should go to their grave without the experience of hearing a purring cat.

CUSTARD CREAMS
Anita Gilson

Ellen Drayton was a small and wispy woman. She lived in Aetherling, an idyllic little village, the sort of place in which people yearn to live. It had a real village green, a delightful little Saxon church, and the kind of good neighbourliness of which most people can only dream.

Ellen was a quiet little spinster, grey haired and self-effacing. She had no talents, except for being useful and staying in the background. She polished and dusted the church but never did anything as artistic as the flower arranging. She mended the hassocks, but never did the embroidery. She was happy to do the drudgework that no one else wanted. She was like a little grey mouse creeping about on little pattering feet.

But she could make custard creams! It was a secret recipe that had been in her family for centuries, passed down orally from mother to daughter - never written down. Ellen's custard creams were renowned. When she made custard creams, Ellen came into her own. They were light and sweet and melted in the mouth.

Aetherling was a happy village, where life was peaceful and pleasant. Nothing ever changed there and no one wanted it to. Then Andrew Pemberton became MP for Midborough, and Aetherling had the misfortune to be in his constituency. Andrew Pemberton was a middle-aged whiz-kid who loathed anything old or unchanging. He had great arrogance and enough wealth and influence to make his older and wiser colleagues fear to cross him.

Andrew Pemberton thought small and pretty villages were useless blockages in the path of motorways and hypermarkets. He began a ruthless programme of destroying them. In vain did villagers and their supporters protest and demonstrate. Pemberton was like a juggernaut, destroying all before him.

To Aetherling's consternation, he had put forward a programme that would annihilate it too. He proposed to close the church, the shop, the police station, the library and museum, the school and the post office. He planned to drive a motorway through Aetherling.

Appalled, the villagers called a meeting and discussed the saving of their village. After much talk, Ellen Drayton stood up. Ina a quiet, hesitate voice, that grew in confidence as she spoke, little Miss Drayton unfolded her plan.

"I think we should pretend we support him, and invite him over. Once we have him here, we can show him how nice life is in Aetherling. He might change his mind when he sees this lovely place for himself, but he won't come if he thinks we're against him."

Everyone was amazed that Ellen Dayton should be so cunning, but they agreed with her plan. So Angela Tansy, the schoolmistress, wrote a letter to Andrew Pemberton , and sent it off.

Andrew Pemberton was surprised and flattered and flattered to find a group of villagers supporting him. He readily agreed to come and talk to them. He was delighted to find himself greeted by bunting, waving flags and cheers. A welcome change from the booing, jeering and egg hurling he usually received. His chauffeur was escorted to the Olde Oak, while Pemberton himself was taken to the Vicarage for tea on the lawn.

Ellen Drayton had surpassed herself. On a little silver tray, especially for the visitor, were dainty plates of delicious sandwiches, a delicate teapot and cup and saucer and a huge plate of her best custard creams. Andrew Pemberton consumed everything with gusto. He was full of praise especially for the custard creams.

Next he was taken on a tour of Aetherling. His lips curled in a sneer. "Very picturesque," he said. "But I'm sure you'll agree that this kind of thing has no place in Century 21."

At this the villagers showed their true colours. They spoke with deep love of village life and raised their voices against turning the country into a mass of motorways and ugly complexes.

Andrew Pemberton's face grew pinched and closed.

"I see that I have been brought here under false pretences. But I can assure you that progress will not be halted!"

He summoned his chauffeur and went home, leaving the villagers angry and depressed. Ellen Drayton said nothing. She went and washed up the tea things. The next morning, Lily Swan, who kept the village shop, was up early to sort out the newspapers. She took a brief look at the font-page headlines, and a cry of joy escaped her.

In a moment she was running down the Main Street, knocking at doors and crying, "Andrew Pemberton's been found dead!"

Sleepy villagers put their heads out of the windows, and then as her words penetrated their befuddled brains, they came out to hear more.

"What happened?" "He wasn't old." "Was he ill?"

It was a mystery, the papers said. He had come home from his visit to Aetherling, one of the rare villages that seemed to support him, judging by their letter to him. His housekeeper had found him on the sofa. Foul play was not suspected, despite Pemberton's unpopularity. His doctor had diagnosed heart failure.

Joy was unconfined. Everyone knew that Pemberton's 'Village Project' would be dropped like a hot potato by other politicians, who knew a vote loser when they saw it.

Ellen Drayton, as usual, said nothing. She made a large batch of custard creams as a celebration. As she followed the ancient secret recipe, she hummed, and a small smile played on her lips.

THE CHARIOTEER
Bryan Oliver

Blikzem was ugly.

Jean-Paul had forgotten – if he ever knew – why he had called the army car *Blikzem*. Understandable because he was only six now and he'd been four when he named it.

But Dieter remembered. When they had occupied the French village, from one of the doorways, had emerged this small boy who had run up to the car and had run his hand over one of the mottled wings.

"Can I have ride, *m 'sieur*?"

"You can, if you ask him nicely," the German sergeant smiled.

Jean-Paul ran to the front of the vehicle and laid his cheek against the paintwork. "Please, *Blikzem*, may I have a ride in you?"

Dieter laughed, "What did you call it?"

"*Blikzem*,' the boy said.

"But why?"

"Because that's his name," the boy said, impatiently. "Can I have a ride now?'

Dieter was only twenty-one but he recognised the futility of asking why a small boy should fall in love the ugliest vehicle in the German army.

"Tomorrow, all right, *mon petit*? Now, we must find a home."

"You can stay in my house!" the boy said emphatically.

"Spread out and commandeer a billet!" the sergeant shouted to the others. "

Then they set off, the boy pulling him along in excitement. At the door of a small stone house Jean-Paul ran in, calling for his mother. He was startled when his mother grabbed him quickly and attempted to close the door.

The German pushed it back. "You are now occupied. You have to billet a soldier of the German army. Do you have a room?"

"We have no room."

"Mama, we have the room where Grandmamma comes to stay," he said anxiously.

Dieter looked down at him and smiled. "Then you had better show me where it is," he said. He took the boy's hand.

'Don't worry, Mama," Jean-Paul said to his mother. "It's all right. I'm going to ride in *Blikzem*."

For Jean-Paul, in 1940, it was as if he had entered into a world of which boys could only dream. *Blikzem* would leap into life and roar like a lion along the rutted country roads with the ecstatic boy on its back.

Whenever the sergeant had to go into the nearest town to report to headquarters or pick up some equipment the boy went with him.

After school Jean-Paul would take a bucket and cloth and wash his beloved monster. Dieter bought him a stool so that he could reach the top of the windscreen. Jean-Paul talked to the car all the time.

The yearning for his father faded quickly from the boy's mind. They had not seen him since 1940 and his mother sometimes cried. Jean-Paul had also missed him at first, but then this dim shadow had no chance of claiming a place against the heroic Dieter who could make *Blikzem* fly down the narrow lanes.

Life in the village returned to its normal peaceful ways. The occupying platoon settled in and drifted lazily into the item of village life. The German soldiers, even helped around the farms.

In such a remote country area, calm brought a false sense of security.

Until the emergency, that was.

It was about seven o'clock in the morning when a hammering on the door awoke all three in the house. Jean-Paul opened his bedroom door. The next moment, the platoon radio operator clumped up the stairs making for Dieter's room. Dieter emerged in full uniform, buckling on his equipment and carrying his sub-machine gun. Then Dieter disappeared in a scramble and Jean-Paul heard him shouting across the village.

Jean-Paul went into his mother's bedroom. "Mama, what is happening?" he asked.

Then he stopped. Leaning out of the back window facing the hill behind, his mother was making peculiar movements with a white cloth.

"What are you doing?" the boy asked.

"Nothing. Shaking the dust. Go and get dressed."

Then Jean-Paul heard *Blikzem's* roar. For a moment he couldn't believe that Dieter would go off on his own without him.

He hurtled down the stairs and ran into the square. Dieter's car was leading a truck with the rest of the platoon on it.

Jean-Paul raced after them. "Diet! Diet! Take me with you."

He just had time to see Dieter turn and wave back before both vehicles took a turn and were out of sight.

Jean-Paul started to walk back, kicking the dust in frustration. Then he heard guns. A continuous fury of gun fire that went on for several minutes, then ceased abruptly. He could no longer hear *Blikzem's* growling roar and realised that the vehicles had stopped. He began to run.

A hundred metres beyond the bend, the road was a smoking chaos. The truck was slewed sideways. Two Germans were lying in the road, the rest were dead in the truck. To the boy's horror, *Blikzem* had ploughed off the road and rammed itself into a tree, the bonnet was crumpled and had sprung open and steam hissed from the radiator. Dieter had stains on his tunic. His head was turned towards him but the blue eyes didn't seem to see him.

The door was hanging open. Jean-Paul banged his fist against the German's knee. "Look what you've done to *Blikzem*!" he howled.

Dieter didn't answer, so he left them both and started to walk back to the tillage, kicking the dirt in his anger. One of the resistance fighters who'd staged the ambush came out of the bushes and called to him.

"Papa!" Jean-Paul shouted.

The man grabbed him, lifted him up and held him.

But then, all he could think of for the moment was the destruction of his beloved chariot. "Poor *Blikzem,"* he burbled, his tears coming again.

As his father set him down and jogged with him towards the village Jean-Paul's tears ceased, dried abruptly by a happy thought. Papa was home. And everybody knew that fathers were good at mending cars.

TAKE A BOY LIKE YOU
Margaret Rose

Alison glanced around the sumptuous apartment and waved her arms in a gleeful manner. "I just can't believe it Joe."

Joe Carter looked at his fiancé and smiled. "You remind me of a street urchin instead of someone recently out of Uni." Glancing down at herself, she had to agree. Her jeans had holes over the pockets and knees, a grey baggy top that had once been white, and a plastic belt that had seen better days. She laughed, her russet hair was in complete disarray, yet she had never felt happier.

"Come on Joe, spill the beans!"

"Whatever do you mean?"

"Did Elsie really just see you in the newsagents and offer us this place, when we hardly had enough money for a bedsit?"

"Well, she heard me laughing with Peter across the counter, whilst I was writing the ad".

"What about?"

"He suggested that I try for a hut on the allotment opposite and I replied that I was going to try the cemetery over the way, but it was closed for stocktaking."

Alison chuckled. "That's what I love about you, your inability to commit to reality. So what was it, a gift from God?"

"Think she just fell for my charm and sense of humour."

Alison jumped up. "Well whatever it was, I for one am very grateful."

Joe bent and kissed her on the cheek.

"That was a bit chaste wasn't it?"

He grinned, "Oh, I wasn't aware you wanted to be chased." He made a lunge for her and she ran squealing towards the lounge door. Just as she reached it, she stopped abruptly. The door was partly open, showing the curved staircase leading to an apartment above. A man was climbing the stairs and turned to look at her.

Joe appeared, "What's wrong Al?"

"That chap upstairs."

"Andre, what did he do?"

"I think I know why that sweet old lady offered you this place – she was desperate."

"You mean I haven't any charm?"

"Please be serious. I think he's a druggie." Her face had a touch of pallor and Joe looked uncomfortable.

"You remember Martin? Joe…the trouble he caused at Uni. And that look…the pale complexion, dilated pupils, unaware of anything around him, that's what I've just seen."

Joe stared at her.

"You never believed in fairy stories did you Al?" He wore a sad expression and her heart went out to him.

"Still, we haven't had any proo…" There was a sharp rap at the door and Elsie breezed in.

"Sorry to disturb you kids, but I'm having a few friends over to dinner tonight and I know they would love to meet you, mainly because they're dead nosey." She patted Alison's hand. "Don't worry, they're nice people and I'll try not to poison you." Elsie grinned. "I'll see you at eight then." And then she was gone.

"You know Joe, it might not be too bad if Andre is invited, and he may well be, he'll have to smarten up, and he can't be all bad, he looks like a slightly older version of you."

"Yes I can see that, in fact, I thought you might fancy him."

"Without wishing to be rude, he gives me the creeps - mind you, if he comes off the drugs, you might have to watch out." She looked around at the lovely antiques, mahogany tables, wall lights, etc. "If these articles are genuine Joe, this place would be worth a small fortune."

"Mmm…and I love the way the sun casts neat little shadows across the room reflecting in your large brown eyes."

She tossed a cushion at him. "Are you taking the mick?"

He was laughing now. "You know our parents will think we've been up to something dodgy when they see this place."

"How could we, with a sweet old lady like Elsie?"

"Oh the time!" they both yelled.

"Come in, come in."

Elsie was in a red silk dress and her neat white hair looked quite resplendent. "These are my friends, Mavis and Laura. Liz could not come, family problems. All women though Joe, hope you can cope."

How smart everyone looked. But he had to ask, "No Andre then?" but never heard the reply as everyone was being seated. Though later, Alison confessed she was certain Elsie had said "No, who?"

"What a pleasure to see such splendid outfits." Joe smiled at the ladies. Alison kicked him gently under the table.

"You old smoothie."

"I'm not a bit toothy!" His face never moved a muscle and Alison laughed.

The food was excellent and laugher echoed around the table. Elsie raised her glass of champagne, bought especially for the occasion. "Welcome, and cheers everyone, here's to many more congenial evenings. Before you go however, today I found a very old photo album in my attic and thought I'd show it to you."

Well preserved, the rich sepia was only slightly faded and as Joe leaned over he could see quite clearly in the foreground the lively, smiling face of Andre, a glass raised to his lips as if to say "Cheers!"

At that precise moment Andre, aka Joseph Lee Carter, was approaching the front door. This time he didn't bother to open it. Now there was no need, his great, great grandmother had the genuine article on the other side of the door. Andre smiled. He knew she would never be lonely again. He considered it a job well done.

First Prize

Samuel Bonner was born in London in 1986. After graduating from London Metropolitan University with a degree in Film Studies and Creative Writing, he signed a publishing contract and released his debut, *Playground*, at the age of 23.

SOMETIMES
Samuel Bonner

Her eyes were a ghost that still haunted him. They had been like two black, precious stones, blazing, glimmering. He could have lived a thousand lifetimes just staring into her eyes.

'Hello Sir. What can I get you?' The waitress asks, thawing him from the memory he'd been frozen in.

'I'll have a coffee and a slice of the peach cobbler, please,' Lawrence replies without assistance from the menu.

When the waitress leaves, he looks out the window. The pavements are blackened with slush from the previous week of snowfall. A few flakes drift now but they won't stick. The sky is clear and an odd purple colour.

When he looks across the table, the booth is no longer empty. Elaine is sat there warming her hands around a frothy hot chocolate, her nose and cheeks red from the cold outdoors. Her hair is a mass of wild, black curls. That's how she used to keep her hair when they were nineteen, and that's how he always liked it. When mid-twenties approached, she began straightening it, despite his protests.

'It makes me look professional,' she'd say. 'Nobody takes a woman with big hair seriously. Especially men.'

Just then, he wants to cry. And in that instant, he's sure that the scent of cinnamon that wafts by him is not from the Danish tray way over by the counter, but from her perfume. It's gone in less than a second, and maybe, well, *maybe* he imagined it. Now the place smells of coffee and bacon, fried foods and the odd gust of car exhaust as customers enter and leave. Tears are in his eyes. Lawrence wants to cry; he's found it to be more therapeutic than alcohol lately, but he also knows that if he starts, he won't stop. Once the tears begin rolling, they have to continue until there's nothing left. That's the only way he's been able to sleep lately, and he's adjusted to the wet pillowcases. To avoid this, he concentrates on her image; he lives for these brief snapshots but also dreads them.

'What if I were to ask you to marry me?' He says under his breath, staring through her transparent outline and at the red cushioning of the booth. Now, the urge to weep is almost uncontrollable. The last thing he wants is to cause a scene, so he grabs the napkin from beneath his knife and fork and dabs at his eyes.

'You're silly,' she responds, shaking her head and laughing.

'Why? Let's do it.'

'You're just going to ask me in this place? Just like that?'

'Yeah.'

'Not very romantic, is it?'

But it was. Maybe she just didn't know it then. Or maybe, the cafe was more symbolic to him than it was to her. It was the place they came after the cinema, where they got their hot drinks after dinner, where they'd share a slice of peach cobbler if she fancied something sweet.

'You haven't even got me a ring have you, Lawrence?' She says with a smile, her head slightly cocked to the side.

He lifts one of his onion rings from his plate and reaches for her hand. She pulls away, laughing. 'Don't put that greasy thing near me,' she says through giggles, 'stop it Lawrence. You're gonna get ketchup on me!'

Something hurts inside of him. It's like indigestion, except he hasn't eaten anything all day.

His face feels numb. Lawrence looks out the window again. He sees himself walking with her on the opposite side of the street, carrying shopping bags full of Christmas presents. He can see the younger version of them laughing, probably at one of his terrible jokes. They walk in slow motion, standing out from the rest of the pedestrians, glowing with that rare, cruel breed of happiness.

They're two fools in love.

'Here you go, Sir,' the waitress returns with his order.

'Thank you,' he tries to say, but his throat is dry and raspy. The waitress gets the implication and smiles, then leaves him to his food.

Lawrence looks at the cobbler. He wonders what he'll see when he takes a bite, and actually becomes fearful of raising his spoon to find out. For a moment, he just rubs the palms of his hands against his trousers like a recovering alcoholic staring down at a shot of whiskey. He goes for the coffee first. After a few hasty sips, the spoon carves through the cobbler. He raises it to his mouth.

'It's not good,' Elaine says, her head bowed, fiddling with her napkin.

He feels like he's been struck with a hammer. This time when he reaches for her hand, there's a real ring on it. He squeezes her fingers, unsure of what to say.

Perhaps there is no need for words. Perhaps silence is the only thing that should be spoken, but still he continues.

'Listen to me, Elaine. We can beat this. You understand?'

Those eyes burn through him; two black, smouldering coals. It's a look he doesn't recognise; in all the years he's known and loved her, he's never seen her face look quite like that before. Then she says four dreadful words.

'Everything has it's time.'

The spoon goes down, some of the cobbler spilling off it and hitting the table. He buries his face in his hands and the tears trickle through his fingers. In his bleary vision, he watches Elaine fade, her image dissipating like breath on a window.

And then she's gone again. He knows he'll probably see her in his sleep tonight, and somehow, that comforts him in a sour way. Lawrence grabs a crinkled note from his wallet and leaves it on the table.

He gets up and starts toward the door on legs that don't feel like his own, and haven't done for quite some time. The cold breeze hits him, the snow flecks his cheeks.

Nothing in the world should have to feel like this, he thinks.

THE LETTER

Helen Silvester

"It's over. I can't do this anymore. I'm sorry."

That was all it said. He folded the paper and left it on the kitchen table, leaving the pen there too. It was a cowardly way to end a five-year relationship but he didn't know how else to do it. He took his keys, discarded his mobile on the side, and left his house. Their house – the one they had bought together.

Today he wouldn't go to work, he would spend the day walking by the sea to clear his head.

When he pulled up at the coast, the sea was dancing, glistening in the morning sun. He saw nothing but the words she would read in a few short hours when she returned from work.

He locked the car and started to walk, lost in thoughts. It was not his fault – he didn't want to get married, at least not yet and he wanted children, of course he did, just not that soon.

She was a sweet girl, eager to please and an infectious laughter. He remembered when they met: he had been sitting across the bar, enjoying a pint while he talked with the lads. He had been struck not by the mass of long curly hair, nor the slender curves that her dress showed off, but by the eyes - deep dark brown in colour. They sparkled at him and at him alone.

They'd talked, he'd kissed her goodnight. Called her, texted her, taken her to the cinema. She'd laughed, sang songs in the night, held his hand, cried when her grandfather died.

He'd listened, she'd listened, she'd helped him when he lost his job, helped him find another, washed his clothes, made polite conversation with his parents, made coffee with cream because he liked it that way.

He looked at the sea and felt the salt on his face, causing his eyes to sting with memories and the sharp wind. For hours he sat there, hearing her voice, remembering how her eyes changed colour when he made love to her, how her hair lay across the pillow in the mornings. He looked at his watch. She would be home by now. In an empty house.

She would take some clothes and stay with her mother, he could hear her saying it. She would cry and probably be angry. Then she would understand and accept his decision. She always did.

He thought of the time when she had first suggested marriage. Of course she wanted a wedding and a family, anyone with a heart as golden as hers would want it. And she deserved it. He tried to imagine who it would be that would one day lie there with her at night as he had done every night since he had known what love was. But he couldn't imagine a face that would make her smile, he did not want to know. Hopefully, never would know.

He closed his eyes and pictured her in a white dress, her cocoa skin glowing and her hair braided down her back. He could smell the white roses that she would carry. He could hear the applause of loved ones joining them in celebration.

He tried to imagine their child. It didn't fill him with fear as it had done last night, or the night before. Now he felt a sense of longing that he couldn't explain.

Like a bullet in the stomach he realised he was not afraid of living his life with her. He had feared so much for so long and never told her. He should have explained and she would have tried to understand. Instinct told him to drive back at twice the speed limit and tell her he had made a mistake. She wouldn't smile and say nothing because she would know that he had a problem. And he would have to make her understand that a problem he had never voiced had been solved without her. She wouldn't understand. She would blame herself, she would call off the wedding. Probably already had done.

He got in the car and drove back. How could he explain? He had thrown it away and now he had to take it back. He didn't want to get drunk with his friends, go home to an empty house, finish the bottle and wonder where life had gone. That was how it would be.

He pulled up at the house. Her car was on the driveway. Had she packed her bags already? Was she crying? Despite the haste to get home he suddenly slowed down, turning his key in the lock, dreading going inside.

He could hear music, she was playing some old tune that they had heard together late at night while he teased her body. It stung his heart and he tried to swallow the lump in his throat.

She was sitting on the sofa, curled up in one of his shirts, her eyes in a book. She looked up to greet her lover, her face breaking into a smile.

"Hey, how was your day?"

He was dumfounded, what should he say, was she winding him up?

"Okay," he said eventually.

"What's up?" she asked him. "You look pale."

"Nothing," he answered confused as he headed towards the kitchen.

"Oh, by the way," her voice trailed after him. "You left the kitchen window open this morning. I closed it because it was a little draughty."

He walked into the kitchen, his skin chilled by the fresh air. The pen was where he had left it; the note was gone. His eyes moved towards a small gap between the fridge and the wall. Inside the slot was the letter that had blown off the table in the breeze.

He lit the letter and watched the paper curl into a few tiny ashes.

He went back and kissed her hair.

"Let's go through the wedding plans tonight."

And he sat down beside her. Happy.

BUILDING BRIDGES
Alison Thompson

Yanking and pushing her temperamental trolley along the aisle, Freda's eyes darted over the serried rows of tins, packets, bottles and cartons impressively displayed. Where on earth had the cereals section gone to? The supermarket manager had obviously been overcome by yet another manic moment and carried out one of his 'reorganisations.' This meant that the items on Freda's list could only be hunted down with difficulty.

A boy aged about eight, with spiky hair and flailing arms, ran zig-zagging down the aisle and collided with Freda's trolley. The screams of a toddler, bored and tired, kicking furiously and impotently in the child seat at the forefront of its mother's trolley, assaulted Freda's ears, while the mother tried ineptly to manoeuvre her trolley around Freda. Half term had certainly begun.

During the school holidays Freda had to grit her teeth and do her supermarket shopping as swiftly as she could, weaving her way amongst harassed parents, bored children and sulky teenagers. She had never been a fan of children and both she and her husband, Les, dead now for 4 years, had remained childless through choice. In Freda's opinion children should be herded into kibbutzes, and kept there until the age of twenty-five at least. After that age there was a faint chance of their becoming acceptable human beings.

Today was definitely not a swift day. The long trailing queues at all the checkouts moved only sluggishly forward. Freda leaned heavily on her trolley while customers unloaded their goods in front of her. Her arthritic hip was playing up today. Like it or not, she would just have to have the operation before long.

Once outside, her few bits and pieces of shopping - after all, how much did one elderly woman and a cat need? - tidily enclosed in her shabby bags, which like their owner had seen better days, Freda paused on the edge of the car park. Where on earth in this vas ocean of cars had she parked hers? She often couldn't remember after emerging from the confusing chaos of the supermarket. Oh, yes, it was somewhere over to the right, near the car wash. Must be careful now. The unexpectedly severe winter had resulted in a period of snow, frost and ice, and consequent dangerous conditions underfoot.

Freda stepped out gingerly. Why on earth had the car park not been gritted? After all, these big supermarket chains were startingly rich and could easily afford to keep their customers safe. Muttering under her breath about the meanness of big business, Freda pushed her trolley slowly towards her small green mini which she could just now see, although it was almost entirely hidden amongst much larger, more ostentatious vehicles.

Car parks were dangerous places. Especially supermarket car parks. Cars zooming up and down and round and round, looking for spaces, cars backing out of spaces, cars suddenly turning into spaces, while customers trundled their trolleys amongst the cars. You needed eyes all around your head, mused Freda grimly.

Without warning a battered – looking transit van backed towards Freda and her trolley, the tyres unable to get a grip on the grubby stretches of ice. She jerked the trolley away, then lost her balance on the treacherous ground and lay spread-eagled, surrounded by her shopping – tins, packets, a couple of pork chops imprisoned in their plastic wrapping, bright, polished apples skidding over the ice – covered tarmac.

"Let me help you up. You went down with one hell of a bump." A broad local accent. Freda squinted upwards from her undignified position on the frozen ground, and saw a young woman bending over her. A firm, gentle hand took hold of Freda's arm, and pulled her carefully up until she was in the sitting position.

"Do you think you've broken anything?" The dark-haired girl took off her denim jacket and spread it over the ice. "Try standing up on my coat, then you won't slip again."

Freda heaved herself up awkwardly and found herself obliged to lean heavily on this youthful Good Samaritan. While doing so, she became aware of a small child valiantly doing her best to pick up Freda's scattered possessions and stuff them back into the bags.

"I'm Mia, and I'm 5. What's your name?" Without waiting for a reply the child picked up a tin of cat food and pronounced: "What a lot of cat tins. You must have got a lot of cats."

Children are so forward these days thought Freda disapprovingly. In my day children simply didn't dare speak to adults so boldly.

"My name is Mrs Lawrence," she replied stiffly, and I have just one cat."

The child's long hair, dark like her mother's swung across her face in the cold breeze. She opened her mouth to ask more questions, but her mother intervened quickly." I think we'll just gather up Mrs Lawrence's things, Mia and then perhaps she'll feel well enough to come back with us for a cup of tea. Afterwards she'll feel able to drive home." From a crouching position she looked up at Freda. "I'm called Jackie by the way. We live just round the corner."

Once on her feet Freda felt shaky, but her legs were functioning. She had clearly not broken anything. Jackie deftly placed Freda's shopping in the boot of the little green car, and all 3 set off slowly for the exit.

A row of colourless, drab terraced houses came into view. Mia skipped ahead along the pavement, miraculously managing not to nose-dive onto the ice. She slid to a halt outside a dark red door with the number 5 imprinted on it.

"This is our house," she announced, grinning, broadly up at Freda. Jackie slipped her key into the lock, and propelled Freda gently through a short, dark hall, bereft of a carpet, then upstairs to a sort of bedroom-cum-sitting room-cum-kitchen where an imitation coal fire glowed easily.

Placing her two bags of shopping on the table by the window. Jackie filled a kettle, popped teabags into two cheerfully decorated mugs, and poured orange juice into a glass for Mia in a few swift movements. Feeling somewhat dazed, Freda found herself clutching a hot mug and wondering how and why she had come to accept this invitation.

Mia sat herself cross-legged on the floor by Freda's chair. "We just live in two rooms at the moment," she announced, taking little sips from her juice. "Because of the water."

Freda looked enquiringly at Jackie. The latter cupped her hands around her mug and sat down at the table. "We were flooded out - you know, six months ago when we had the terrible floods here," she explained quietly. "Lots of people had to leave their homes. The landlord's still wrestling with the insurance people. That's why we're living upstairs. Downstairs is a total mess."

Freda gazed at her speechless. Of course, these streets in this low-lying part of town near the river had all been under several feet of water. In her mind's eye, she saw again the almost unbearable pictures on the TV, many of which were flashed around the world - of houses almost submerged, of surging, hostile water, of people and their pets being rescued by boat, of desperate people being picked off rooftops by helicopters.

"We went to live with my dad for a while," continued Jackie. "He's on his own now since my mum died, and he's got a spare bedroom. Lee, that's my partner, and Mia and me, all shared one room. Lee - he's a bricklayer - had to travel to work on three buses."

A small hand plucked at Freda's sleeve. Two dark eyes gazed steadily upwards. "What's your cat's name, Mrs Lawrence?"

Freda placed her empty mug tidily on the bedside table that appeared to be doubling up as a sort of all-purpose coffee table.

She's called Daisy," she replied, finding to her surprise that she was actually managing to smile at the child. Smiles did not come easily to Freda.

Bending her head downwards again, Mia fiddled with the laces on her small red shoes.

"We had a cat once," she said slowly. "He was called "Alfie, and he was my friend. He got drowned in the flood."

A silence descended on the cluttered room, broken only by the small shuffling sounds of Mia's shoes on the worn rug. Gazing through the window at a leafless chestnut tree in the nearby frozen park, a chastened Freda reflected that here was one child who should definitely not be sent into a kibbutz.

MR DONALDSON
David Warren

Isn't that Kenny over there? Walking on the other side of the High Street?

Kenny. Well I never! He's very smart in those clothes, and he's got really short hair. Suits him. Hang on, he's rushing. Why's he got that folder under his arm? On business? He still walks in that funny way: leaning back, extra straight! He looks as if he's about to tip over, just like that time when we were coming off Snowdon together and he lost his balance. When I ran back to help him, Kenny was grateful, I could tell.

Those were good trips to Wales we all had: everyone desperate to go on Night Nav, and idiot Johnnie T taking a frying pan up Tryfan, and bonehead Scoffa stuffing two ready meals down his face every evening; and then old Rick getting a bloodied nose from a woman because they all dared him to kiss her. Wonder what's happened to old granny Rick?

I don't want to go and hold Kenny up, not if he's busy. He's going to think it's odd though, if he's seen me here looking at him and I don't say hi. He's a big young man, powerful-looking chest: in great shape. But, of course, he'd be delighted to see me: he wrote that nice email saying that he was back in town for the game; 'It'd be really nice to meet you again,' he'd written. I wonder if he still plays? What a player he was; when he ran with the ball, those great curly locks of hair of his flying behind him, and the intense concentration on his face. All the others used to look up to him, hanging on his every word as he'd gather the fifteen around at half-time. 'Keep spinning it out wide,' he'd say in his resonant voice. And then the hat-trick, when he was drafted into the football team. That was a magnificent chip for the winning goal, standing there, arms outstretched, waiting for the others to come and jump on him in celebration.

Perhaps I *should* go and greet him, just quickly? I am looking pretty smart myself today and my cologne's still strong. Also, I probably won't see him again for a while. But, hang on, he's walked past me now, I'd have to run and catch him up. Besides, if I'm not careful I'm going to be late for my appraisal. Trust that to get in the way. Still, thank God Minty was writing the report for my class. It was lucky I'd had the brains to write *him* a glowing review; I'm sure he'll have returned the favour. Even if he hasn't, he won't have said anything bad. Not like one of the new guys would have done if they'd been assessing me. Us old chaps have really got to stick together. Just look what happened to Graham Burns, getting kicked out and left without a pension. What's the world coming to, political correctness gone mad?

Hello. Kenny's going into that posh 'Dino's' cocktail place. Maybe I'll just pull over here and decide on a plan; this traffic's not moving anyway. Kenny liked my classes. He'd sit quietly at the back looking embarrassed, as the other boys messed around and made jokes about sex. He was a good, hard-working kid.

What should I do? I can't stay here, but it would be great to catch up with him. Perhaps I could call the secretary and rearrange my appointment with Dr. Walsh. He wouldn't mind and I could say my mother had been taken ill again. Yes I'll do that. It'd be nice for Kenny and me to catch up over a drink. There was intelligence about Kenny. I'd be teaching Plato and he'd sit there calmly, staring at me, before cocking his head to one side, reddening and nervously asking something clever.

Since I'm parked here, hadn't I better go into the bar? I'm going to look silly if Kenny comes out and finds me lingering on the kerb. I could go to 'Dino's' and easily make it seem like it was an accident that I was popping in; I'd just stroll up and touch him on the arm, no, on the shoulder, and say something like, 'Hey, it's Kenny isn't it? I don't believe it! I remember you from school.' No, better: 'I remember you from our trips to Wales.' Yes, perhaps I should do that.

He was such an understanding kid. When I got that erection as they were all changing, he didn't join in the laughter and jeering, he just looked down at his feet and coloured. He'd never take part in the arse banging jokes of the boys either. He'd always gaze at me in sympathy when Murphy and his pal, Harris, were making blow job gestures during House Prayers.

I'll wait until this crowd of tourists get clear of 'Dino's,' and then I'll go over. It'll be great to see him. After that time in the mountain hut, when we'd got back from the hike ahead of the others, I know he'll want to meet again. If only that Carlson hadn't brought the rest of the boys back then! Something would have happened, I know it. Me and Kenny. It was obvious even when he was a new boy: his little puppy face looking up at me with those searching hazelnut eyes. Kenny and me. He was so beautiful. I knew he wanted me.

Hang on, he's coming out. What's this? He's with a girl? No. It's nothing, it's nothing, they're only friends. He'd always had female *friends*. Of course, a guy like that was popular with the girls, but they hadn't meant anything. Shit. Kenny and the girl are coming this way, towards me! They're holding hands. Fuck. Can they see me? What if they see me? No, I don't think he's noticed. Thank God, he's simply walking by, he's simply walking on by.

WHITE CHRISTMAS

Joyce Anderson

'Married!'

John Cowan felt shock and excitement ripple through his body at his daughter's unexpected announcement.

'Are you thrilled then?' Angela asked, happiness laced with uncertainty in her voice.

'Of course! And your mum will be thrilled, wait till I tell her the news, she's out feeding the hens.'

'I'm so happy, Dad. You've not met David yet, but we'll be with you for Christmas.'

John struggled to take in all the news. Not only was his little girl married, but she was coming home all the way from South Africa, where she'd worked as a teacher for five years.

'Is it snowing there?' she asked.

'Not yet,' replied John, glancing out of the farmhouse window. 'But they reckon we'll have a white Christmas.'

Angela ran out of change, and the line went dead.

John went straight to the kitchen and put the kettle on for his wife coming back. A cup of tea would help settle their nerves.

Two days before Christmas, John and Mary Cowan met their daughter Angela and her new husband at Gatwick Airport. A telegram confirming the time of their arrival had been delivered shortly after the phone call.

The flight from Johannesburg had been a long one, but their daughter looked as fresh as the day she'd left. Her blonde hair was longer, curlier and her cheeks glowed like shiny red apples.

A tall young man with dark brown hair and a pleasant face stood beside her, beaming at the two of them. Angela turned and introduced him to her parents.

'Mum...Dad... this is David and he's a vet. He ran his own practice in Durban and we met in the summer.'

'Delighted to meet you both,' said David in a crisp South African accent. He shook both Mary's hand and John's, then explained: 'We had the wedding ceremony on the beach – it's all on film, so you'll enjoy seeing it later. Love at first sight I'm afraid!' He stared wistfully at the charming old couple before adding, somewhat guiltily, 'Sorry you people weren't there. It's so very far away.'

John Cowan shifted uncomfortably while his wife Mary seized the moment and hugged the shy stranger. Brushing all the awkward feelings away in three simple sentences: 'What's done is done, lad! You're family now. Welcome home!'

The Cowan's place was an hour and a half from the airport. A light covering of frost from the day before, which hadn't melted, coated the trees and hedgerows. Spiders' webs hung from the barn doors where John's tractor lay, and all the animals came out to greet them. Hens ran alongside the big jeep and Mary quickly touched the horn to alert two sandy coloured goats about to cross their path.

'I never knew you kept goats!' exclaimed Angela, admiring them. The smallest one was heavy with kid and looked about to give birth. The tallest, the male, stared back at her curiously.

'That's Holly and Mistletoe,' her mother replied. We bought them this year from the farmers' market and we're hoping to breed them. This will be Holly's first birth.' She glanced nervously at her husband. 'Looks like she'll drop her kid any day now, and I'll be busy in the kitchen what with Christmas dinner an' all to prepare.'

David's voice came from the back of the jeep, putting their minds at rest as he said calmly, 'You mustn't worry Mrs Cowan. You've two extra pairs of hands now. I can help John with the delivery if there are any complications, and your daughter can help in the kitchen.'

Mr Cowan pulled to a stop in front of the old farmhouse and gave his wife a hug.

'There, what did I tell you? If we all pull together, we can have the best Christmas ever!'

Letting go of her, he glanced in the mirror above him and spoke to the loving couple in the back. 'It's not been easy this year, what with the government cut backs. This place has become a little run down I'm afraid. The extra pairs of hands you mentioned will be a real blessing, if only for a few days.'

David helped Angela out of the jeep and as they came round the front of the vehicle, he noticed the out buildings. One looked empty and dilapidated. The two goats made for it and disappeared.

On Christmas morning, Angela rose bright and early to help her mother with the rest of the preparations for Christmas dinner. She peeled the potatoes, parsnips and sprouts, then basted the huge turkey and set the table. The fairy lights from the Christmas tree in the corner cast a colourful glow over the whole room.

David brought down two bottles of the best South African wine from his cases, and placed them on the dining table beside the crackers covering the damask tablecloth. Red napkins fanned the wine glassed and tall white candles rose out of the decorative holly and mistletoe holder.

Outside, the pink sky that had greeted them all at breakfast, suddenly became dark grey and heavy with snow. The first flurry came as Mrs Cowan lit the candles and turned on the radio. Christmas carols were sounding out across the farm through the open kitchen window, when all of a sudden the little bulb suspended from the old barn roof, went out. John Cowan cursed under his breath, as he tried to deliver Holly's kid in the dark.

Last time he looked, the feet were sticking out and it was going to be a difficult time for the young goat.

'Where's your father?' asked Mrs Cowan, about to dish up. The Christmas meal was cooked and ready to serve. 'Thank God for gas cookers!' she muttered quietly to herself.

The farmhouse had plunged into darkness but for the light from the Christmas candles which Angela carefully distributed throughout the house. The carol singing stopped abruptly as the radio went dead and the whole countryside fell still and silent in the power cut. Only the noisy bleat of a goat could be heard coming from the barn across the way.

David grabbed his coat, a small bag and a torch and rushed out through the back door.

'Bring lots of hot water!' he shouted back to the women.

Snow had quickly covered the countryside in a white blanket, and through the falling flakes the young vent crunched his way over to the out building. John Cowan was pleased to see him and even more relieved after the young kid was delivered safely into his arms. Using his skills and cutting tools from his bag, David managed to make an incision wide enough for the little goat to pass through easily. The two women brought basins and buckets of clean hot water, and when the little kid was cleaned up and able to breath, it lay writhing in the straw. Everyone watched anxiously.

Suddenly in the glow of the torch, it struggled to stand up on its weak little legs, and gave a plaintive bleat. Holly licked him all over, and together they stood side by side on the warm clean straw. He was pure white and full of life.

The lights came on again and the family returned to the warm farmhouse to enjoy the wonderful festive meal the two women had helped cook. David helped pour out the wine and after two glasses announced cheerfully the couple's good news.

'We're not here for a few days, you know. We're home for good! I sold up my practice in Durban and I reckon with the help of a local builder, we could convert these two out buildings into a proper place for all these goats you're going to breed. We could make our own goat's cheese as well and sell it at the farm market.'

John and Mary were delighted with the young couple's news and thrilled at the prospect of their new venture. 'Let's drink a toast to the future, to all working together, and the new little goat... Hey, what will we call him?' asked John rising from the table to look out of the window. 'Let's think,' he said, pausing for a moment. 'His mother's called Holly, his father's called Mistletoe...'

'Snow!' they all cried out in unison, and then burst out laughing at the realisation they had all thought of the same name at the same time.

It really was a white Christmas. The best ever.

WORLD WITHOUT GUILT

Steve Belzak

George made his way across Threadneadle Street, heading to the Underground. If it was hot above ground, it would be sweltering in the confines of the Tube. Normally, he wouldn't be going this way, but his boss, Bob Clayton of FFOPIR Associates, had invited him to dinner.

George's route took him past the by now inescapable large screens beaming out the official news and commercial advertisements. One, featuring a voluptuous young woman with dark hair caught his attention.

"Do you suffer unnecessarily from guilt feelings? I did, for no good reason – until I discovered "Heaven's Peace," the new miracle pill from NHS-Pfizer-Kline-Bayer-Toshiba."

The woman leaned forward, the camera focussing on her soft, moist lips and bright, pleasant eyes, pupils dilated. *"Why be a victim of the past? Live for the future. You'll never know peace until you discover Heaven's Peace."*

The screen moved to another topic, and George resumed his walk in the shimmering air.

At Bob's West London apartment he was let in by an attractive woman in her thirties, at least twenty years younger than George.

"I'm Elizabeth," she said, "but my friends call me Beth." Her smile was seductive. "You can call me Beth if you desire, George."

George was struggling for air.

"If you want," said Beth, "you can freshen up. The bathroom's in there. You'll find plenty of towels."

"Thank you, Beth," he stammered as he made his way into the bathroom, locking the door firmly behind him.

At dinner they sat at a long, polished table, George at one end, Bob at the other, with Beth seating herself next to George.

Bob dominated the conversation. "George here is my finest commodity futures trader. He works hard, is a financial genius and makes us and him a *hell* of a lot of money."

Beth glanced at George, a look of awe and admiration in her eyes. "But there's a 'but', isn't there Bob? I can tell from your voice."

"Yes, there is Beth. He won't listen when I tell him he should trade food futures."

"I'm sure there's a good reason."

"Yes, there is. Futures trading can push up the price of commodities, and that opens up the possibility of people going hungry."

Beth poured George a drink. "I told you there was a good reason, Bob. Here, try this George. Let's enjoy ourselves instead of talking business."

Next morning in the office, George was a little hazy in his recollections of the previous evening, but he *did* feel a wonderful sense of inner calm. Even when Bob's secretary phoned him to come up to Bob's office, something that usually generated acid indigestion, he felt at peace. He listened to Bob outline his plans for the future of the firm, and joined him in a cup of latte.

After George had left, Beth appeared from the next room. "I did it, Bob, but I'm not sure this is wise," she complained, and flung a piece of paper at him. It was the user information guide for Heaven's Peace, which Bob read.

"Dosage: Always dissolve in water or other liquid before taking Heaven's Peace.

For mild symptoms of guilt, one x 1mg tablet per day with food.

For more serious symptoms, take as directed by your medical practitioner, but in any event no more than four x 1mg tablets per day.

Warning: Side effects may include but are not limited to mood swings, irresponsible behaviour, blurred vision, depression, elation, headaches (inc migraine), dizziness, impotence, retarded ejaculation, permanent penile erection (in men), haemorrhoids, violent outbursts and urinary incontinence.

If you suffer any of these symptoms consult your doctor immediately!"

"So how many did you give him?"

"You requested twelve; I gave him twelve. Like last night."

After several weeks, George gave into Bob's demands and transferred to the Food Futures Unit, where he excelled. Earnings increased, and the financial press began to recognize FFOPIR Associates as a big player on the food futures market. However, the mainstream media also picked up what they believed to be the firm's deleterious role in denying food to the poorest people on Earth, by pushing up prices.

So it was that on another sweltering day the following summer, George found himself walking across Threadneadle Street, but this time he was going to the local studios of Guido-Fox Political News.

Again, the gigantic screens were churning out news and infomercials. George, brought up in an Evangelical Church of England home, couldn't avoid the Archbishop of Canterbury talking about Heaven's Peace:

"The Gospels tell us that Jesus Christ came to take away our sins, and the guilt for our sins, but this doesn't negate the role of human medicine in the Atonement, especially for faith groups who don't have faith in the need for atonement. Heaven's Peace is, I believe, God's provision of salvation for those who don't accept His provision at the Cross."

The advert ended with an upbeat rendition of Beethoven's Ninth and the words:

"NHS – Pfizer – Kline – Bayer - Toshiba – Giving you Competition through Monopoly."

George enjoyed the hostile interview, concluding by denying that it was his fault "failed states like Somalia, Bangladesh and the Irish Republic are unwilling to compete for food on the open market, which is the essence of a free and prosperous economy."

He then went to Bob's house, was greeted by Beth with a kiss, and went to Bob's study. Bob was surprised to see him, and even more surprised to see George point a gun at him and pull the trigger.

George and Beth had sex on the study floor while Bob's lifeless eyes looked on. Afterwards they watched TV, which featured one of the Archbishop's critics.

"What he doesn't realize is that there's a difference between a *clear* conscience and *no* conscience."

But he was greeted with derisive laughter from the interviewer, and from George and Beth.

FREED SPIRIT

Robert Aston

Except for that one occasion, Bill never showed any interest in his wife's drawings. He'd flicked through her sketch-book, feeling free to criticise, as is often the case with those who can't do it themselves.

'Can you only draw *that tree*?' he'd scoffed.

'Why not?' she'd retorted, defensive and affronted. 'That's how you build up a feel for your subject.'

'Huh!' He'd tossed the book down onto the table, the best page bent over and creased.

Things came to a head on May Day Eve, an evening warm, a full moon blazing in a bright silvered sky.

She stood quite still, savouring the scent of bluebells. Earth and sky were united in one timeless moment. Somewhere out of sight, Pan was playing his pipes, just beyond the range of human hearing.

Her eyes strayed to her beech tree, silhouetted against the last faint glow of the departing sun.

On a sudden impulse she ran towards it, casting off the clothing that confined her. As her brassier parachuted into a holly bush, she gasped with delight at the cool caresses of the evening air.

In spite of her forty years, her body was well proportioned and it gleamed like alabaster as she reached her tree.

In bright patches of moonlight, golden-starred Celandines lay scattered among the roots. Wrapping her arms around the trunk she hugged it to her, breasts and belly savouring the hardness of the bark. Stars glistened amongst green leaves now turned to black.

She allowed her knees to buckle, encountering a protrusion. Bill had sawn the branch off many years before and she'd been sketching it ever since. Bark had now grown over the stump, leaving just a tiny hole surrounded by wrinkles.

Having kept her panties on, she pressed down against the hard unyielding bulge. In complete control, she clamped her thighs around the trunk and swung her sandaled feet up off the ground. She was flying through a forest... a witch upon her broomstick... a Valkyrie riding her winged steed.

For the first time in her life, she felt fully ALIVE. *This* was what art could do for you... fuse body, mind, spirit.

A voice shrilled out in the darkness: *'Good Grief. Mabel. Have you finally taken leave of your senses?'*

Even as she recovered from the shock, she couldn't help but smile at her husband's quaint turn of phrase. But she felt no shame as she pressed closer to the bark.

'Actually, I've just come *to* them,' she retorted. Irritated by his indignant silhouette, she issued a challenge that she knew he'd refuse, 'Why don't you strip off and join me?'

'No way!' he snorted. 'Come inside, before the neighbours see you. That tree's for the chop as well.'

She felt a quiver rippling through the bark... or perhaps her sensitised skin. Torn from the tree, she was dragged back into the house.

'God knows what the neighbours must be thinking,' Bill called after her as she stomped up the stairs to the bathroom. 'That tree has really got to go,' he added, returning to his novel.

Mabel was glad to wake up. She'd been having one of those dreams that are so disturbing that the waking mind recalls every detail. She'd been standing beside a grave, stark naked and very male. He'd felt brisk rubbing all over his skin. Yet the women who were scrubbing him down showed no interest in his body: apart from getting it clean. It was as though he was dead already: as he soon would be… by The Triple-Death to bring life back into the fields.

At the blast of a horn, a rope was passed around his neck and the women hauled enthusiastically on its ends. As he'd gasped for breath, the sharp edge of a leaf-shaped sword sliced into his throat. With his huge lungs now filling with blood, a stone axe smashed into his forehead. Then she woke up.

'What was that irritating buzzing noise?'

The chainsaw! *Jim was cutting her tree down.*

Leaping out of bed, Mabel rushed out of the house and down to her precious tree. Bill was perched near the top of his ladder, cutting through a branch. Screaming in protest, she reached the foot of the ladder as the limb sagged and dropped. Attempting to catch it, she tripped over the power lead and fell against the ladder. Bill missed his footing and lost control of the saw. Swinging down, it sliced into his side. He toppled back, the cable tightening round his neck. He hung suspended: his blood showering down onto Mabel's upturned face. Finally, he plummeted to the ground. The screaming stopped as his forehead struck a stone. Mabel recovered from her trance. 'The Triple Death,' she screeched, 'and serve you bloody-well-right!'

As Mabel rushed indoors to phone for the police, her husband's blood soaked into the earth. Passing the roots of his intended victim, it reached an ancient land-surface where a few scattered teeth were all that remained of the shaman. As his body had rotted, an un-chewed beech nut from his last sacrificial meal had sprouted. Something of his essence had survived, accumulated by successive generations of beech trees until awakened by the attentions of the woman. By trance-journeying to other worlds, the shaman had died knowing that this was not the end. His only regret had been his abstention from knowing a woman. And now he'd been granted that pleasure. Moreover, someone *else* had endured The Triple-Death, releasing him to join the spirits of his tribe.

Someone else could watch and wait as a thousand years dragged by. Someone else could feel the water table sinking away. As he freed himself from his prison, the shaman was sure of one thing: try as they might to stop it, inter-glacial warming would continue to plague his people.

NOTHING could stop it.

Not even the gods.